Bonita

SPIRIT
of the CIMARRON

Bonita

by KATHLEEN DUEY

PUFFIN BOOKS

Published by the Penguin Group

Penguin Putnam Books for Young Readers,

345 Hudson Street, New York, New York 10014, U.S.A.

Penguin Books Ltd, 80 Strand, London WC2R ORL, England

Penguin Books Australia Ltd, Ringwood, Victoria, Australia

Penguin Books Canada Ltd, 10 Alcorn Avenue, Toronto, Ontario, Canada M4V 3B2

Penguin Books (N.Z.) Ltd, 182-190 Wairau Road, Auckland 10, New Zealand

Penguin Books Ltd, Registered Offices: Harmondsworth, Middlesex, England

Published in the United States of America by Puffin Books,

a division of Penguin Putnam Books for Young Readers, 2002

Published simultaneously by Dutton Children's Books

1 3 5 7 9 10 8 6 4 2

TM & © 2002 DreamWorks LLC

Text by Kathleen Duey

All rights reserved

Puffin Books ISBN 0-14-230095-0

Printed in the United States of America

The characters and story in this book were inspired by the
Dreamworks film *Spirit: Stallion of the Cimarron.*

Chapter One

The night I was born three grooms watched over my mother. They pillowed her stall with deep, clean straw and brought her warmed water to drink. She was a beauty, with white and gold in cloud shapes across her back and belly. My father was famous, people said. He won races in grand cities back east before a Texian rancher bought him and brought him west to San Antonio. When it was time for me to learn how to balance a sidesaddle and rider, I was brought into the barn. I did my best. I arched my neck and I lifted my hooves high when I trotted. Maria loved me, I think. I know I loved her.

The scent of the earliest wildflowers was on the wind. Inside the barn, Bonita was restless, pacing in her stall. There was room for four short steps, then she had to double back.

Bonita switched her tail as she turned, impatient, listening for the sound of light, graceful footsteps crossing the road from the rancho's adobe house.

Where was Maria?

Bonita lifted her head over the stall gate to see out the wide doors at the far end of the barn. Maria *would* come this morning.

Bonita was sure because the groom had awakened her early. He had brushed her white coat into silk, then oiled her hooves to blacken them. Maria always made sure that Bonita was groomed perfectly before they went anywhere.

Bonita listened.

The wind was carrying the sound of voices as well as the scent of wildflowers this morning. Bonita straightened her ears, listening, then lowered them in disappointment. It was just the two men who had stayed over the night before.

Bonita didn't know either one of them—or their horses. She was getting tired of all the strangers in the barn. There had been a parade of men and their horses lately. And all of the men had been tense and grim.

Some of them wore buckskins, others wore dark suits with starched white collars buttoned around their necks. A few had Mexican serapes with colors shaded like rainbows. Most wore old homespun shirts.

They all sat on the porch for a day or two, talking until late at night with Maria's husband, James. Their horses all ate fast and then dozed, waiting, as though they were used to this kind of uncertain stopover.

"What do you make of it?" one of this morning's men asked as he came into the barn. He jerked a thumb back at the house.

"Not sure," his companion answered.

They saddled their horses without brushing them, still talking, their voices low and urgent. Bonita stamped a forehoof, wishing they would hurry and leave. She hated all their tight-lipped talk. They made her uneasy.

Bonita lashed her tail impatiently. She had been waiting for Maria to come, not these grim-faced men. Maria's sweet, clear voice and her gentle hands always helped soothe the terrible uneasiness the men brought with them.

Bonita tossed her head. She longed for Maria to take her out for a long gallop today. And she knew that as long as these men were in the barn Maria wouldn't come. She didn't like any of them. Maria's stiff posture and quietness around all her husband's recent visitors made that very clear.

"I know this much," the first man was saying as he swung up into his saddle. "It won't be over until the Texians surrender to the Mexican government."

"Which means it'll never be over," the second answered bitterly.

They rode out, ducking beneath the door beams, then spurred their horses into a gallop. Bonita heard the hoofbeats fade as they turned onto the long road back toward San Antonio de Bexar.

Bonita welcomed the relaxed silence after they had gone. In the corner stall, Banjo, an old Morgan gelding, stretched his neck and yawned, showing his worn, yellowed teeth. Across the aisle, two pasture mares waited to give birth. They often groomed each other across the stall rails and stood near each other, even though there were rails between them. It was obvious they were old friends.

Bonita didn't really know them and it wasn't likely she ever would. Once their colts were born and were a few days old and sturdy on their legs, the mares would go back out to pasture, probably for good. Very few horses actually lived in the barn.

Tall, lanky Gavilan was dozing in the next stall. Gavilan was Maria's husband's favorite mount. He was calm and polite and Bonita liked him a great deal. He never reached over to steal her hay; he never whinnied or pawed the floor of his stall. When he got restless and paced, he was quiet about it.

Bonita shook her mane and settled into listening for footsteps again. More than anything, she wanted to hear Maria's gentle voice and to get out into the sunshine for a gallop. She loved to pound along with Maria's cape and skirt—and her own mane and tail—flying in the wind.

But the sound of light footsteps did not come and after a few minutes, Bonita swung back around, pacing her stall again.

Chapter Two

*E*ven in the midst of all the trouble, and all the terrible things that happened afterward, I can remember the first time I saw Raphael. It was on the way to town, and I remember wondering how it felt for those horses, to gallop so free, so fast.

Sudden footsteps, light and graceful, made Bonita lean against the stall gate, watching the door.

Finally!

María swept into the barn, her long dark skirts brushing the dust. Her shining black hair was pulled back in a blue ribbon. A broad-brimmed hat shaded her milky complexion; cotton gloves shielded her hands.

María was dressed for a long ride! Overjoyed, Bonita whickered a greeting.

María smiled. "Buenos días, La Bonita. Where's Juan?" She turned and called out the stable hand's name.

He shouted an answer from somewhere out behind the barn.

"You look like you're ready for a run, pretty one," she said to Bonita, then touched Bonita's forehead. "I told Mrs. Gaus I would help her cook for the Texian Volunteers at the Alamo today." She tugged gently at Bonita's long forelock. "The men won't even consider backing down. I would think the Mexican government would decide we were too much trouble and leave us alone." She laughed, but it was a sad sound.

Bonita arched her neck, then pulled away. She could tell María was upset and it only made her own impatience worse. She paced her stall once more, turning sharply to come back to the gate. María's light touch usually soothed her, but this morning was different. Bonita was so eager to get outside that she struck the dirt with a forehoof and shook her mane.

"Sí, Señora?" the groom asked, coming into the barn.

"Saddle the mare for me, please," María said.

Juan nodded and went to the tack room. He came back carrying Bonita's bridle and the black leather sidesaddle María preferred.

Bonita came out of the stall the second the gate opened and the groom laughed a little, pulling her halter to make her stop. "She's eager for a run."

María smiled. "So am I. I am so weary of all this sad news about the war. I wish the Texians and the Mexicans could simply live side by side in peace."

Juan did not answer, but he set his mouth into a tight line. The worry in María's voice bothered Bonita, making her even more restless. Bonita tried to stand still while Juan settled the folded blanket, then the sidesaddle, on her back. He eased the cinch

9

tighter, then jerked it hard to make sure she had let out all her breath.

Bonita hated to have him jerk the cinch like that. It startled her every time, even though she knew it was coming.

She laid back her ears, but allowed herself no other reaction. Bonita knew María was proud of her stable manners—and didn't want to endanger that opinion.

Bonita stood still as Juan fussed with the saddle, straightening the stirrup strap. It was hard to stand quietly. She had not been out of the stall in days. She could scent the warmth of the morning, the perfume of the sacahuiste grass.

Juan finished his work quickly. In minutes Bonita was tacked up, her bridle reins lying in a loose loop over her withers. Bonita followed the groom out of the barn and stood completely still while he let María brace one foot on his bent knee, then step up, turning deftly to sit down in the saddle, facing him. He held the single stirrup steady while María crossed her ankles, then placed her left foot in it.

Gavilan whinnied a farewell and Bonita answered him. She could feel Maria shifting the cloth of her full skirts, settling her thighs against the Y-shaped tree of the sidesaddle.

"Ready, Bonita?"

Bonita felt the subtle shift in Maria's weight that meant she could start off. A gentle pressure on the right rein told her which way she was to go.

Bonita turned, her hooves clopping hollowly on the hard soil as Maria guided her down the fenced lane. It was wonderful to be outside! A whinny from one of the pastures made Bonita turn her head. A tall, angular sorrel mare was staring over the fence.

Seresa.

Bonita tossed her head, wishing she could go play with her old friend.

Bonita had been born four days before Seresa. They had learned to use their long legs by playing together. They had run long circles, veering sharply along the fencelines, racing each other as well as they could within the boundaries of the pasture.

But Seresa had never been brought into the barn.

Bonita saw her sometimes if Juan or the other stablemen saddled her in the barn to ride into town. She was used to carrying ranch hands when the cattle were gathered.

Seresa whinnied once more and Bonita tossed her head to look back.

Just then, María shifted in the saddle, adjusting her dress. Then she pressed her left boot down harder, steadying the sidesaddle's single stirrup, centering her balance.

Bonita knew what all this meant. When María leaned forward again, a definite and decisive movement, Bonita was ready. She broke into a canter.

Bonita fell into the rhythm of her stride as well as she could with María on her back. María rode well—with none of the loose-armed flopping around that Bonita noticed in other women riders. Even so, it was still hard to gallop gracefully. At first, it had been hard to gallop at all.

There were often people on the main road. Bonita saw a dun horse coming toward them, ambling along at a trot. His coat very nearly matched the yellow-brown of the road dust. The rider was a man and Bonita envied the dun for an instant. Men sat astride, with one leg dangling down each side of their mounts. Their saddles had two stirrups.

Balancing a man's weight was an easier task, Bonita knew. Long before Maria had ever ridden her, a man named Gonzales had trained her. He had taught her to pay attention to the little shifts of a rider's weight and the pressure of the reins on her bit.

As they got closer to the dun, Bonita's envy faded. She could see the salt-stiff curls of old sweat in his coat. His saddle was nicked and scarred from rough work in hard country.

Maria reined Bonita in a little and they passed the cowboy at a collected canter. Bonita lifted her forefeet higher and higher, and she felt Maria sit straighter in the saddle. The man tipped his hat and the dun flicked his ears forward, a quick twitch, a gesture of greeting that Bonita did not return. Ruffian cow ponies like this one rarely saw the inside of a barn.

Maria laughed a little once he had passed. Bonita

knew why. They had both been showing off—for a dirty cowboy and his rough-coated horse! There had been no parties or parades lately and Bonita was sure Maria missed these chances to dress up as much as she did. She tossed her mane and felt Maria's warm hand on her neck. Maria laughed again, then let the reins out.

Bonita rose back into a gallop. Her hooves made a wonderful hollow clatter on the packed earth of the road. It was still nothing like a full gallop, but it felt grand to extend herself even this much. Maria began to sing as she often did when they were off and alone like this. She had a high clear voice.

Coming around a bend, Bonita saw two tall, lean-looking horses in the distance. Their riders had dismounted. The two men were struggling with their pack animal. The burro kept rearing, dragging backward on its rope.

Maria reined Bonita in sharply, pulling her back to a walk. As they slowly got closer, the problem became clearer.

Bonita stared. It was awful. The load piled onto the burro's back was obviously too heavy. The poor animal could barely stand under the weight. Still, one of the men had a whip and he was lashing at the burro's rump, trying to drive him forward.

Bonita danced to one side, flinching at the loud popping of the whip. How could the poor burro stand it? It was not his fault the men had put too much weight on his back.

Bonita heard Maria make a sound of dismay and knew she was upset, too. Gentle Maria never allowed any of the ranch horses to be handled like this. Any groom that was caught being cruel would have lost his job instantly.

Suddenly the burro reared, striking at the whip like it was a poisonous snake. Bonita watched, astonished, as he bucked, wrenching himself to one side. The pack straps gave way and the heavy load fell to the ground.

Furious, the men forced the burro to a standstill. Together, they reloaded the brave little animal. The instant the men stepped back, the burro reared again.

Bonita pulled at the bit, wanting to gallop again, to get past the awful scene. Maria held her in.

One of the men was trying to drag the dusty little burro forward. The burro nearly sat down, bracing his hindquarters. He refused to take a single step.

Arguing, the men divided the load, tying two of the big bags behind their own saddles. The burro lifted his head. Once the load was manageable, he obeyed the lead rope willingly, carrying the still heavy packs without complaint.

As Bonita neared them, the men mounted and started off. Maria suddenly loosed the reins and threw her weight forward. Bonita lunged into a canter, catching up quickly.

"I will buy that burro from you," Maria called out to the two men. They turned in their saddles to stare at her.

"I will buy the burro," she shouted.

The men looked at each other.

"I am quite serious," Maria assured them. She was sitting very straight in the saddle and Bonita lifted her head high.

The tallest shrugged and smiled mockingly at María. "You think you could handle Paco better than I do?"

María didn't answer.

Both men wore dark coats and looked filthy. Bonita felt María's tension through the reins and she readied herself to gallop away if either of the men tried to approach.

Suddenly, without another word, the men turned away and rode off, taking a wagon-wheel track that led out across the open country.

Paco looked back at Bonita, flicking his ears the way the dun cow pony had. Bonita arched her neck and extended her muzzle in a friendly gesture. She could not imagine what it would be like to live with such terrible men.

The lead rope tightened and Paco had to turn away, trailing behind the men's mounts, valiantly carrying the heavily loaded packsaddle without complaint.

Bonita sidled. Paco was dusty and small—and smelly—she was sure. But he was braver than any horse she had ever seen. He didn't deserve to have such a cruel master.

María sat stiffly in the saddle, holding the reins uncomfortably tight, until the men ahead of them were well away. Then she loosened the reins and leaned forward again.

"I want to go home, Bonita," she said aloud. "Back to *la sierra*, the mountains that disappear into the sky. But James will not leave his precious Texas."

Bonita turned toward San Antonio trotting, finally breaking into a canter. María rode quietly, her singing stilled. Bonita knew she was upset over the brave burro, too.

After a time, Bonita lengthened her stride. Her breathing settled into a cadence with her hoofbeats and every deep breath lifted her heart a little.

It was a glorious day. The air was full of the scents of early spring. On both sides of the road the land was green from the recent rains, and the sky was bright blue and endless.

María's skirts belled and billowed when a rush

of wind hit them. Bonita held herself steady against the startling flashes of dark cloth at the edge of her vision. The quick movement might have meant some wolf—or lion—was leaping toward her haunches, trying to drag her down. But of course it didn't.

During Bonita's first days carrying a rider, Gonzales had carried an old shirt. He had waved it around Bonita's belly and back until she had understood that she was safe with a rider on her back. By the time María had ridden her for the first time, Bonita had known better than to shy at fluttering cloth.

The road curved between the Alazan hills and Bonita extended her neck, stretching, pulling just a little at the bit. María held her steady.

Bonita surged forward anyway, knowing she shouldn't.

María reined in harder. The straight metal bar of the bit was pulled tight against Bonita's tongue.

It hurt.

Bonita forced herself to slow down, the pressure easing as she obeyed. Staying at a half-gallop, Bonita only gradually began to feel less desperate, more content with the controlled gait María was allowing her. The long road into San Antonio had been rutted with wagon wheels during the winter storms. Bonita kept to the side, galloping along the road's edge, placing her hooves where the spring grass ended and the worn dust of the road began.

They passed the San Antonio de Valero Mission on its little rise. Beneath the stand of cottonwood trees, Bonita could see the men in buckskin pants and homespun shirts digging ditches and piling rock against the walls. They weren't planting corn or trees as she had thought at first. Bonita lifted her head. She could smell the peach blossoms in the little orchard beyond the mission.

Breathing hard, Bonita slowed to a canter, then stopped as María reined her in. "I wonder if Jim is at the Alamo today?" she said aloud. Bonita turned to face the mission, savoring the east wind that lifted her mane.

María stared a moment more, then wheeled Bonita back onto the road, back into a canter. As

Bonita started around a long curve in the road, changing leads, she was startled by the deep, rolling clatter of galloping hooves. Then she saw the horses.

They weren't on the road. They were off to the west, close to the river, galloping hard, their necks stretched out, their hooves a blur as they pounded along.

Bonita turned her head to watch. They wore no tack, they had no riders. Four cowboys rode hard behind them, whooping and swinging long lariat ropes, driving them onward. She could hear them shouting back and forth. "Head off the palomino," one of them kept hollering. "Turn Raphael or he'll lead them all the way to Mexico!"

It was obvious which horse he meant. At the front of the herd was a young stallion with a coat that shone like Maria's gold earrings in the sun. He was a length in front of any of the others and gaining ground fast.

Bonita wanted to keep watching, but Maria was leaning forward, urging her onward. The road turned again and the horses were out of sight behind them. Bonita listened, her ears swiveled backward, but the sound of the whooping cowboys faded quickly.

The dusty streets of San Antonio de Bexar were crowded with horses and wagons. Bonita knew the turns; they had been to Mrs. Gaus's house many times before. As she trotted up, she saw that the tables set beneath the cottonwoods were full of women, as usual. They sat talking as they chopped onions and garlic and stirred huge pots of stew that cooked over open fires.

"There you are!" Mrs. Gaus said when she saw Maria.

"Is there more news about the war?" Maria said, sliding to the ground. She looped Bonita's reins loosely over the rail.

"Only that the Mexican army is still coming," Mrs. Gaus said. "No good news. Not for us."

Bonita stood at the hitching rail as they walked away from her. There were beautifully braided and groomed ladies' mounts tethered on either side of her and she knew that she should be polite and greet them as well as she could ... but she couldn't stop thinking about the horses she had seen.

What did it feel like to gallop like that, flat out, without a saddle or rider—or pasture fences in the way? Had the gold-colored stallion managed to out-race the cowboys?

Chapter Three

*M*aria began to come out to the barn
more often. I think she liked sitting
quietly, away from all the men who were shouting and arguing in the house. Her husband saddled Gavilan one morning and rode away. I
never saw Gavilan again, or James . . . I don't
know what happened to them.

One day, Maria came to the barn at sunrise.

"Just bring her out and tie her for me please,"
she instructed Juan.

The groom opened the stall door and Bonita

eased forward, waiting for María to step back. Juan led Bonita in a tight circle, then tied the lead rope to the top plank of the stall gate.

"Look what I have, Bonita," María said. She held out a brown paper parcel. Bonita extended her muzzle, breathing in. She could smell the dusty indigo dye on the ribbons she knew were in it. She rubbed her muzzle gently on María's shoulder, grateful. She loved to stand quietly while María's gentle hands worked through her mane and tail.

María began to hum as she combed every tiny tangle from Bonita's tail. Then she began the long, careful task of making rows of tiny, perfect braids, weaving the ribbons in and out.

Bonita closed her eyes and let out a long breath. It felt nice to be fussed over. María had done her mane and tail many times—it usually meant a party was coming up.

Bonita hoped that was what it meant this time. María and her husband often rode side by side to some other rancho to celebrate a wedding or a birthday. Bonita liked walking along the moonlit roads beside Jim and Gavilan. Gavilan was steady and kind.

Bonita liked the dances, weddings, and quinceañeras in San Antonio de Bexar, too. She liked the crowded courtyards and the candle lanterns lighting the walkways. She loved the children. They often gave her apples and admired her snow-white coat.

Bonita looked down the wide aisle toward Gavilan's stall. It was still empty.

Maria followed her gaze, took a quick, deep breath, and then went back to work on Bonita's long white tail. Bonita liked it. The dangling ribbons tickled, but in a pleasant way, not like flies or a stray piece of straw.

Bonita lowered her head and closed her eyes as Maria began work on her mane.

"I am worried," Maria said, talking to herself as she often did when she and Bonita were alone together.

"No one will have a party," Maria went on quietly. "They are too scared about the war. But I will do this anyway. We will pretend the world is as it should be." After a long time, she started humming again and Bonita was glad. The tension in Maria's voice had made her uneasy.

After the braiding was finished, Maria stood at Bonita's shoulder, leaning against her. Bonita could smell the flower scent that was as much a part of Maria as her gentle hands and voice.

"I want the happy days before the war to come back," Maria whispered. Bonita turned to touch Maria's hair with her muzzle.

Maria stood very still for a long moment. Then she stepped back. "Juan?" she called. "Will you saddle the mare now?"

"There are soldiers everywhere," he said in a respectful voice. "People are so afraid of the war they are leaving town with everything they own. Perhaps it is not safe for a lady to ride alone?"

Maria glanced at him. "I will not let fear of this war take everything from me, Juan. Not everything. I won't. And I am needed at Mrs. Gaus's."

He did not answer but went about his work. Bonita stood as quietly as she could, nuzzling at

María's shoulder to show that she felt the tension, that she understood something was terribly wrong.

Finally ready, they stepped out into the sunshine. Juan helped María into the saddle and they were off.

The ranch road was damp. It had rained in the night, just enough to settle the dust. Steam rose from the backs of the pasture horses. Their coats looked rough.

Seresa whinnied her usual greeting and Bonita answered her, as always. A quick breeze flared the ribbons in Bonita's tail and one of the pasture mares shied away from the fence. Seresa blew a breath out of her nostrils, a low sound of disapproval.

Bonita lifted her head, trying to look back. But it was too late to see whether Seresa had been impatient with the shying mare, or with Bonita for having fancy braids.

As they turned toward town, Bonita saw a line of wagons in the distance—all headed toward her. When they got closer, Bonita felt María's weight shift a little—but it wasn't a signal to canter. María was merely sitting straighter in the saddle, raising her head.

Bonita did her usual part, arching her neck and prancing as the wagons approached. As the first of the line passed them, Bonita concentrated on lifting her forefeet high and sidled to swing the braids in her tail.

Then she noticed that these wagons were different from the ones they usually saw. For one thing, the drivers' benches were crowded. Instead of a single wagoner, there were whole families. Some of them had several older children in the wagon bed, perched on top of a jumble of goods.

None of the people were smiling or admiring Bonita's braids or her snowy coat. They all looked frightened. Bonita lost the cadence of her trot and slowed a little. Maria urged her forward and after passing six or eight more wagons, she nudged Bonita into a canter.

The wagons kept coming as the road swung close to the river. They were *all* oddly loaded, Bonita saw, piled with a mixture of things—cloth, chairs, boxes, and trunks. The children rode in silence, their eyes wide, glancing ahead, then back toward San Antonio.

When Bonita's long strides carried her past the last of the wagons, she felt Maria's tension ease.

"They are running away from the war," Maria murmured. "I wonder if we should do the same, Bonita?" Then she sighed. "James would never go."

As the rattle of the oak wheels faded behind them, Bonita's canter loosened and rose to a hand-gallop. Maria did not rein her in. She stayed on the smooth road edge as always and let the ground pass beneath her hooves.

After a long while, as they passed the men working at the Alamo, Maria reined Bonita in. She turned in the saddle and shaded her eyes with one hand, staring. After a long moment, she sighed and shifted her weight so that Bonita would go on.

They cantered onward, following the road into San Antonio. The river was high and Bonita welcomed the cool water brushing against her belly as they crossed.

Then, just before they turned onto the lane

where Mrs. Gaus lived, Bonita heard the sound of pounding hooves behind them.

She sidled, trotting at an angle, looking back. There were horses—a lot of horses—trotting together down the road. But they weren't acting like a pastured herd—or even like horses carrying riders usually did. They were lined up straight, like rows of garden corn.

María reined Bonita aside, then pulled her to a halt. Bonita stared as the horses thundered past them. They looked weary. Their ribs showed and their hip bones stood out beneath their dusty coats. Still, their heads were high and their eyes were fixed on the road ahead.

Bonita blinked. The riders all looked alike. They were all wearing similar coats and hats and all their clothes and faces were caked with road dust.

María used gentle but insistent pressure on the reins to straighten Bonita, to get her walking away from the road, away from the grim, weary horses. Bonita obeyed, but she was puzzled. Why would anyone ride like that? And why did their horses stand for it? They were too close together. If one of them stumbled, several would be hurt.

The sound of hooves dimmed, then faded as the horses trotted past and went on. María signaled another turn and Bonita felt a little silly. She knew where they were going. María shouldn't have to tell her.

There were three little girls walking up Mrs. Gaus's lane. Bonita made her way around them, watching their eyes go wide when they saw how beautiful her mane and tail looked, how lovely María was. Bonita raised her head a little, but all the joy of showing off was gone.

María's uneasiness and the overloaded wagons on the road had disturbed her; the rows of exhausted horses bothered her even more. Bonita felt anxious. It was like smelling smoke from a distant fire, or hearing wolves howling in the distance. She didn't understand what the danger was, but it was close. And it was coming closer every day.

Chapter Four

The most terrible and painful times can lead to good things. I did not know it then—everything was so tense and uncertain—but everything that happened was in some ways for the best. . . .

Bonita awakened in the dark. There were unfamiliar scents in the wind that whined against the adobe walls of the barn. She flared her nostrils. She could hear the mares across the aisle shifting and whickering to each other. Banjo, the old Morgan, snorted and stamped a hoof.

Bonita wished that Gavilan was there, with his calm alertness—but he wasn't. If Maria's husband had gone to the Alamo, he had not come back yet.

There were hoofbeats on the road and distant thudding sounds like lightning striking, miles away. The hoofbeats got louder, passed the barn, then stopped.

Bonita stood in the dark, shivering even though it was not cold. She heard someone pounding on the rancho door, then muffled voices. Then nothing at all.

The night returned to its usual sounds.

Mice rustled in the barn straw.

The wind gusted outside the door.

Then the hoofbeats clattered to life, passing the barn again, fading back up the main road to San Antonio. Then she heard a distant popping, a scatter of gunshots? Was someone hunting? At night?

"Bonita!"

It was Maria's voice.

An instant later, Bonita heard footsteps over the sound of the wind—then her stall gate was flung wide. María was suddenly beside her, looping a rope around her neck, pulling at her.

Bonita came forward, her head high and her ears flickering back and forth, trying to make sense of what was happening. María never rode at night, not alone.

María led her outside, the wind whipping at the loose white gown she wore. "Bonita, it's beginning," she said, leaning for a second against Bonita's neck. "There's gunfire from the Alamo."

For another moment María stood close, then she stepped back. "Juan says some of the soldiers are raiding the ranchos, taking the horses."

María slipped the rope off Bonita's neck and stood back. "Go on! Run!"

Bonita stood facing María, her heart pounding, her legs trembling. All her instincts told her to run. But run *where*?

"Go!" María slashed at the air with the rope.

Bonita leaped backward, startled, the sandy soil gritty beneath her hooves. She turned as María swung the rope a second time, gathering her weight, glancing back toward the barn. If there was danger, she should go back to her stall now. She wrenched herself around to face the wide doorway.

"No!" María shouted at her, waving her arms, her voice desperate. "Go! Get away!"

This time the rope stung her hindquarters and Bonita lunged away from the pain. Nothing made sense. Why would María drive her away? But she was suddenly galloping without knowing where or why, pounding down the ranch road in the dark, her braids and ribbons streaming in the wind.

At the end of the ranch road, Bonita slowed, looking around wildly, the sounds of distant gunfire sifting through the windy darkness. It was too dark. There had been a quarter moon earlier, but it had set.

Hoofbeats behind her made Bonita whirl around, her mane flying in the wind. The pasture horses were pounding toward her. Had María set them all loose? Bonita wheeled around to gallop with them. As they fanned out onto the road, she followed.

Some of the horses swung toward town, some

away. A few kept going straight, running across the road without turning at all. Bonita plunged to a stop, then galloped off behind those headed toward town.

She had never gone the other direction on this road, nor had she ever, in her whole life, struck out across open country. She could probably find safety at Mrs. Gaus's house. The Gaus family knew her. They would return her to María when the danger had passed. In front of Bonita, one of the mares stumbled in a wheel rut and crashed to her knees, squealing in terror and pain.

Bonita faltered, swerving to miss the fallen mare. She glanced back to see her rising, scrambling upright, then recognized her. Seresa!

Bonita managed to veer off the road, whinnying frantically, whirling around in a circle as the other frantic horses swept past. Seresa answered her and lunged back into a gallop. Together they went on after the others.

As they fled through the dark, the gunfire got louder. Near the Alamo mission, the sound that had seemed like distant lightning strikes from inside the barn began to shake the earth beneath Bonita's hooves.

When the lead horses rounded a bend and saw the night ahead of them flickering with bursts of fire, they slowed, then stopped. Then they stood, breathing hard, dancing in nervous circles.

Bonita was trembling. Seresa, limping a little, came closer and touched Bonita's neck with her muzzle. Bonita turned to breathe in the scent of her old friend, grateful not to be alone. She moved closer, until their shoulders touched. Together they turned to face back up the road—staring at the darkness that suddenly had settled over the Alamo.

Her sides heaving, her legs still shaking, Bonita tried to understand what had happened. Maria had been afraid for her. But why? And what good had it done for Maria to chase her away? The flashes of light and the loud sounds came from the guns, she was sure. Guns killed. Any horse knew that. Guns killed deer and wolves and they killed men.

Maybe she wouldn't make it past the mission into town. Maybe she couldn't get to Mrs. Gaus's house. Bonita took a step toward home. Then she looked back, tossing her head. Seresa watched her, but didn't follow. Her friends from the pasture were all standing close around her.

A booming echo from the Alamo was followed by a ragged chorus of shouts, then more gunfire. Bonita took another step. It made no sense to stay here. But she was afraid to be alone, in the middle of the endless darkness.

A sudden explosion of hoofbeats made Bonita whirl around. Before she or any of the others could react, lines of horses were trotting toward them through the night.

"*Hay caballos!*" came a shout. "Horses!"

Then other voices joined in.

Startled, Bonita spun, half rearing, but it was too late.

The lines of horses wheeled and turned as a single voice shouted above the others. Bonita dodged and plunged, but every direction she faced was already blocked with a line of horses standing so close together that escape was impossible.

From the corner of her eye she saw Seresa rearing, striking out at the horses, startling a gelding into dancing aside. Seresa lunged forward and made it through the line, her hoofbeats receding as she galloped away. Terrified, Bonita tried to follow her, but the men closed ranks and she had to turn back.

Another shout rose above all the noise and men suddenly appeared, on foot, carrying lariats. They spoke in low, soothing voices and Bonita turned toward them, expecting help.

The sudden slap of a lariat on her neck startled her. When it tightened in a single, cruel jerk, she knew these men were not to be trusted. She reared and the lariat tightened, dragging her down again. She tried once more to run and was hauled back around to stand still, shaking and scared.

In minutes, all the horses had been caught up. Bonita thought she heard Seresa's whinny, but couldn't see her in the milling mass of men and horses. Men's voices tangled with the horses' squeals in the dark. Bonita was dragged to one side, the lariat tightening until she could barely breathe.

"This one shows up like the moon," the man

leading Bonita said. "A perfect target."

"I'll trade," another man said from behind him. "She looks highbred. Fast."

Bonita trembled while the lariats changed hands. Without warning, she felt a blanket on her back, then a saddle. One man held her head while another jerked the cinch tight. She could feel the blanket doubling under, wrinkling unevenly beneath the saddle tree.

"Hurry!" someone shouted. "Mount up!"

Bonita turned to face the voice and felt a heavy hand clamp down on her lower jaw. A bit was jammed into her mouth and the bridle was pulled over her ears. It was too loose and the bit clanked against her teeth. Then something happened that startled her so completely that she stood stock-still, astounded and afraid.

The man who had saddled her pulled a knife from his belt. With deft, quick strokes, he cut off her braids, leaving only a ragged fringe of mane as the ribbons slithered to the dirt. He cut her tail, too, taking off the braids close to her skin, leaving it shorter than a newborn foal's. Then he vaulted into the saddle.

Swaying beneath the sudden weight of a rider, Bonita stared at the twisted braids in the road dust. María had tied those ribbons with such care. Bonita felt hollow, remembering how pale and sad María had looked in the moonlight. Nothing was right. Would it ever be right again?

"Ride!" the man screamed.

Bonita felt a sharp sudden pain in her flanks and instinctively jumped forward to escape it. The man in the saddle jerked her to one side and then back, handling the reins with brutal strength. Bonita stumbled, then righted herself as she joined the galloping mass of horses headed straight toward the sound of guns.

Chapter Five

*T*hat night was terrifying. All the horses were shaking with fear. I could only try to live through one moment, then the next. No wolf, no mountain lion, nothing has ever scared me as badly as what the men called the Battle of the Alamo.

Bonita could only gallop awkwardly at first. The man was twice Maria's weight. And it was terrifying to see the dusk-blurred shapes of the horses galloping on either side of her; she could smell their fear. It was madness to gallop this fast, this close together in the dark.

Bonita suddenly realized that she *could* see a little now. She lifted her head. The sky was getting gray. Sunrise was not far off.

"The south wall!"

The horses in front of Bonita veered off to one side. She followed, helpless to do anything else. And when the horses in front of her slowed, then stopped, she could only do the same, wincing at the terrible pressure of the bit that hung too low in her mouth.

"Wait for my order!" came a shout.

Bonita heard men repeating the phrase backward through the lines so that all could hear.

Trembling, her sides heaving, Bonita stood still, afraid that any movement would bring another jerk on the reins, or the spurs in her flanks. She heard horses whinnying, but none of them was Seresa so she did not bother to answer. The whinnying died down quickly—too quickly, amid grunts of pain. Bonita could imagine the aching jaws and bruised flanks of the horses foolish enough to make noise.

Bonita looked at the horse next to her. He was

a tall bay gelding, thin from hard work. His eyes were closed. Bonita stared. Her whole body was shaking with fear. How could he possibly be dozing in the middle of all this?

Bonita kept glancing at the bay. When he finally did open his eyes the weary emptiness in his stare frightened Bonita almost more than the gunfire. It was as though he was staring through her at something so terrible that he had to close his eyes again.

During the darkest part of the night, the sound of gunfire had faded, but with the light it swelled again, the shots coming closer and closer together.

As the sky lightened, Bonita could see that she stood near the back of the many lines of horses and men. Behind them were ranks of burros hitched to what looked like giant guns. Farther back, more burros were loaded with heavy bags tied together on packsaddles. As Bonita scanned the lines of men behind the burros a movement caught her eye.

One of the little gray-coated burros was backing up, shaking his head as a man added another bag to his load. Once it was tied on, the burro refused to move. He reared, striking out with his forehooves like a stallion in a fight.

Cursing, the man removed one of the bags. Around him, there were shouts of sharp laughter. Bonita was pretty sure it was Paco, the brave burro she and María had seen, but her rider was pulling her roughly to one side and she couldn't see.

"Form up!" someone yelled.

Bonita felt the spurs jab her sides. She bolted forward to escape the pain, but instantly met the crushing pressure of the bit. Trying to do what her rider wanted, she slid to a stop, then turned to the right when the bay did, then halted again when the reins tightened.

"Ready!" came a shout. *"Listo!"*

Bonita saw the weary-looking bay's eyes widen in fear, edged in white. The horses were suddenly silent—not even the sound of breathing rose from their ranks. Bonita could feel a painful tension in the horses and their riders.

"Charge!"

Bonita tensed, ready for the wolf's-tooth pain of the spurs. But when it came, she bolted forward. This time, her rider let her go. The lines of panicked horses pounded over the ground together, sweeping onward like summer thunder.

The bay galloped valiantly, his legs flashing in a powerful rhythm. Bonita matched her stride to his, managing her rider's weight better now, keeping up. Maybe, if she just did what the others did, the man would stop hurting her. Maybe, if she didn't anger him, if she did her best...

A rumbling explosion overhead made Bonita shy and she stumbled, crashing into the bay. She staggered aside, fighting the pressure of the bit and terrified by the screams of men and horses in front of her. The bay galloped desperately on without flinching and Bonita sprang forward, fighting to keep up.

In front of her, a man suddenly clutched at his chest, then slumped sideways, falling from his horse. The animal charged onward and Bonita could only leap over the fallen man, desperate to avoid trampling him.

Now the shouting was everywhere, on all sides, overlaying the thunder of hooves and the sound of horses' sobbing breath.

A fresh round of gunfire rang out and there were more screams. Another explosive roar passed above her. Bonita jerked her head up and felt a quick streak of pain trace her shoulder. She plunged to the side and heard her rider curse.

A second later there was an explosion that deafened Bonita. Her rider was shooting, she realized, through the fear that pressed at her from all sides. He was shooting right over her head. Bonita longed for her quiet stable, her old life, Maria's soft voice.

A second shot rang out from between Bonita's ears. This time, she held herself steady and kept going. She could see the walls of the mission grounds now. There were flashes along them, like flaring candles in the dawn-light. With every flash came an explosive roar. The bay squealed and dropped back suddenly. In the same instant, Bonita's rider slid to one side, then pitched out of the saddle.

Stumbling, confused, Bonita kept going. She had

no choice. The horses on all sides of her had not slowed. Bonita kept pace in the ranks, empty stirrups flapping against her sides. Every stride brought her closer to the adobe wall of the mission grounds.

Then, without warning, the horses in front of Bonita slowed, rearing and plunging as the headlong gallop came to an end. Some of the men were dismounting, running forward, firing their weapons.

All around Bonita, the ranks were coming apart. The horses galloped off to one side or another. Bonita stood trembling a second, then whirled and galloped back in the direction she had just come, leaping fallen men and horses, the bridle reins looped loosely on her neck.

The thudding roar of the giant guns shook the ground again. Bonita stopped, shying away from the din, wheeling around to face the adobe wall. Rifles flashed and a man near Bonita fell forward, then lay still upon the ground.

Bonita spun, turning back to the cannon. Just then a resounding bray rose over the clamor of the fight. Bonita saw Paco. He was standing with his legs jutted out to brace himself against the dragging pressure of the rope around his neck.

The burro was carrying a huge load of the round cloth bags. Bonita watched as the man leading him gave up forcing the proud little animal closer to the cannons and began to unload him where he stood, sprinting a few steps back and forth, carrying the heavy bags.

The burro stayed still as a stone until the man had taken the last of the bags and turned to carry it to the cannon line. Then he bolted forward, making his way across the field, cantering as fast as he could through the men and horses. His path was nearly straight, like a horse who knows the way home.

The burro was leaving this place, Bonita realized. He was free and headed away from the noise and pain.

"Paco!" the man shouted. "Paco, you useless, stubborn . . . !"

As the man cursed and shouted, Bonita shook her ragged mane and burst into a gallop. Ignoring the wild flopping of the stirrups and the battle that raged around her, she gathered herself and jumped, sailing over a stack of cannonballs, landing neatly on the far side of the line.

She pounded past the man who was still shaking his fist at Paco and kept going, galloping after the burro.

Chapter Six

Paco helped me when I desperately needed help. He seemed impossibly brave to me then, impossibly clever. He began as a friend and has remained so for as long as we have known each other.

Paco never once faltered. He made his way around men lying belly-down in ditches firing at the Alamo. He skirted wagons that carried supplies without coming close enough for anyone to notice and catch him. Bonita followed him, terrified and grateful.

Within minutes, they were on the fringes of the battle. Not long after that, they were headed away from the fight. Paco led the way and Bonita followed closely, her whole body still vibrating with fear.

Her shoulder ached and stung. She could smell blood and knew it was her own. But she had been lucky. The wound hurt, but not enough to make her limp. She was not lame and the blood would soon dry. That was the main thing, she knew instinctively. She did not want wolves to smell fresh blood and come to investigate.

As the sounds of the battle grew dimmer, Bonita looked back, hoping Maria was safe at home, that Seresa had escaped and was grazing in a sunny pasture somewhere, and that the bay had lived and would never have to face another battle. Bonita was looking back, with her head turned, when Paco stopped suddenly.

Bonita heard the clip-clop of his small hard hooves pause and barely caught herself before she ran into his dusty hindquarters. He turned his head to look at her.

Bonita could see him taking in her chopped-off mane and tail. She felt filthy and was sure her white coat was streaked with dirt and blood. She shook herself, then regretted it instantly when the loose stirrups thudded against her bruised sides.

The burro was standing in an odd position, his neck extended and his whiskered muzzle pointing upward. His nostrils flared and closed with his breathing. He lifted his head and brayed, the sound ringing out. Then, after a moment, he started off again.

Bonita wasn't sure what he had scented, or why he had brayed. But he seemed to know where to go and that was more than she knew. So she followed.

They walked in single file until the sun was high overhead. Then, finally, Paco headed down a long slope that ended at the river. Bonita waded into the shallows and drank gratefully, letting the cold water wash some of the dull, leaden taste of gun smoke from her mouth.

Then the burro led the way back up the bank and started walking again. Bonita followed, glad to have him take the lead. Even with the rifle fire far behind them, she felt shaken, as though the whole world had changed around her.

They stopped to graze where the new grass was deepest. Bonita managed to eat around the bit, but it was uncomfortable. The crumpled edge of the saddle blanket was starting to rub painfully, too. Bonita knew it would soon wear her skin bloody.

Late in the afternoon, Paco found another path down to the river and they drank again. When the wind shifted, toward evening, it brought the distant sound of guns. So the battle was not over. Bonita shook her mane to rid herself of the memories of what she had seen.

Bonita never wanted to see another battle. She never wanted to hear men and horses screaming again. She wished once more for her safe, quiet barn and the sound of Maria's gentle voice. She moved closer to Paco and he flickered his long ears, but did not seem to mind.

Paco led Bonita along the river until the sky darkened. Then he chose a place in a shallow valley to sleep. Without any hesitation, he pawed at the hard dirt, turning in a slow circle before he lay down with a grunting sound.

Bonita looked at the dirt. There were sharp little rocks mixed into the soil. She pawed once or twice, then gave up. She was so weary. And lying down with the saddle would be awful.

So Bonita stood up to sleep, something she had done only rarely in her stall. The saddle cinch dug into her belly and the steel bit turned cold as the night settled in around them.

Bonita was miserable. She dozed fitfully, waking to hear a rustling in the bushes on the riverbank. Paco woke, too, and got to his feet. He moved to stand between Bonita and the sound.

The rustling began again and got louder. Bonita tensed, trying to scent the animal that was making the sound, but the river was upwind and she couldn't.

Paco stood solidly, his front legs set wide. He lowered his head and Bonita looked down at him, amazed. He was ready to protect her. She was twice as tall and twice as heavy, but he was willing to put himself in danger for her.

The rustling stopped, then started again, bursting into a frenzy.

Two young does exploded out of the bushes, a skunk scuttling after them, stiff-legged and angry. The deer bounded away without looking back, leaping in arcs into the dark.

Paco and Bonita backed up, giving the skunk enough room to strut in a circle, scratching at the dirt with her claws, arching her back, furious at being disturbed. Bonita held her breath, hoping the skunk would calm down.

The furious little animal glared at Bonita and Paco, even though they hadn't been the ones to disturb her. Then, as though she had to punish *someone* for being rousted out of her warm predawn nap, she lifted her tail like a flag and released a short burst of her powerful scent.

Paco and Bonita turned in the same instant, bumping into each other. Bonita dodged to one side, but so did Paco and they ended up facing each other.

They tried to get out of each other's way, and ended up swaying back and forth, their heads low, trying to figure out which way to jump. Finally Paco managed to get past Bonita and she whirled around to follow him up the path.

They hadn't been sprayed directly, but Bonita could still smell skunk on her own coat. Paco's woolly fur had absorbed even more of the eye-stinging stink. If they stood still, the smell rose around them like an invisible cloud. So they started walking, even though it was barely light enough to see.

And they kept moving, trying to get away from the smell that clung to them. It was nearly dawn, Bonita saw as they topped a rise. The sky to the east was turning gray. To the south she saw the road that led home. She stared at it for a long moment, then began walking toward her barn. She wanted to find María. She wanted this awful saddle taken off her sore back.

Paco brayed at her.

Bonita stopped and turned to look at him.

He could come with her. She was sure of that. María had admired his courage and had wanted to save him from his cruel master. María would take Paco in—especially if she knew he had helped Bonita escape the battle. Bonita nickered, lowering her head.

Paco lashed his stumpy tail back and forth and Bonita knew he was having trouble deciding. She could not understand why. What did he expect would happen if he just wandered in the hills? Prairie wolves would find him, or he would starve in the fall when the grass died.

Bonita turned toward the road again. She was grateful to Paco and she wished him well. But she didn't want to face any more danger. She was going home. Paco lowered his head. He would follow.

Starting off slowly, Bonita quickly realized that every cut and scrape, every saddle sore, the wound on her shoulder—everything that had hurt the night before, hurt twice as much now. Paco was favoring one back leg just enough to make his gait uneven.

The road was deserted at sunrise and Bonita was glad. There was no sound of gunfire and she was grateful for that as well.

Moving slowly, she led Paco along, turning onto

the narrower road that led to the rancho. Her pace picked up a little as they got closer.

Everything was going to work out. María would see what a brave and good burro Paco was, she was sure. She would call Juan and he would come running to help.

Bonita would even share her stall with Paco until María decided where he should live. There would be corn to eat and Juan would wash their wounds. Bonita flicked her shortened tail at a fly and realized how ugly she must look. María would be so upset ... so angry ... and ...

Bonita stopped in her tracks, staring at the barn and the house beyond it. Something was wrong. It took her a moment to figure it out, but when she did, all the excitement inside her collapsed.

María was not here. No one was here. The ranch was empty. The front door swung free on its hinges, squeaking in the wind. The pasture gate was gone, torn from its place. Bonita walked closer and caught the scent of ashes.

She looked into the barn. A fire had gutted the

adobe building. The stall rails had fallen, thinned and blackened into fragile sticks. Bonita blinked. The back half of the building had collapsed. The little room that had held saddles and bridles was open to the sky.

Bonita walked a few steps toward the house. Fire had been there, too. The walls were blackened and cracked. Worst of all, no matter how hard she tried to find the slightest trace of Maria's scent, she couldn't. The heavy odors of smoke and ash had completely erased it. Bonita felt weak. Nothing was left. Who had done this? *Why?*

Paco let her walk back and forth, following her; then, when she finally stopped, he nuzzled her side and began to chew at the leather cinch.

Bonita lowered her head, closing her eyes. She was exhausted and scared. If Maria wasn't here, what would she do? What could she do? The idea of being captured and forced back into the sound of the gunfire made her legs shake.

When Paco backed up, dragging the saddle from her back, she was startled into lifting her head.

Having the painfully tight saddle and the wrinkled saddle blanket off her back was wonderful. She shook to straighten her coat. Then she touched Paco's shoulder in thanks.

Paco shook his wispy mane and lashed his tail back and forth. He lifted his face to touch Bonita's cheek with his muzzle. He nudged her, then stepped back.

When he turned to lead the way back down the road, Bonita hesitated. Then she lowered her head sadly and followed.

Chapter Seven

R *aphael seemed to be like the wind, like the clouds. He went where he wanted to go. He seemed to belong in the open country. I didn't, not at first. I felt small and scared.*

Bonita walked as though her legs were made of wood. The ill-fitting bridle chafed at her cheekbones and the bit was a constant discomfort, tapping at her molars with every step. Her coat itched where the saddle had been. She longed to be brushed, to have the sweat salt washed away with buckets of sun-warmed water. She longed for her stall, the shelter of the barn roof over her head.

Paco turned toward San Antonio de Bexar on the main road and for a few minutes, Bonita thought he was going to guide her back into the town. The idea both scared and comforted her. But then he veered off the dirt road and started across open country.

Bonita whinnied anxiously, pushing at the annoying bit with her tongue. Then she waited for Paco to stop and look at her. He did not. His short tail switching side to side, the burro just kept going.

Bonita looked behind herself. The road wasn't far. She could still see it. Maybe María would come back to the rancho. But maybe not, too. The sound of the crooked house door creaking in the wind echoed inside Bonita. She recalled the familiar smells and scents of her home—scoured away by the sour smell of burned timbers.

Paco made an impatient snorting sound and Bonita turned to see that he had stopped, finally, and was staring at her. She shook her close-cropped mane and swayed, trying to decide. She took a step toward him. The instant he saw that she was moving, he turned and led the way again.

Bonita followed Paco, but the farther they got from the rancho where she had been born—had always lived—the more uneasy she felt.

She nibbled the grass when Paco stopped to graze, chewing around the bit. The early grass was tender and delicious, but she kept lifting her head, looking back toward the river. Her nervousness would not fade.

Would the long lines of horses and riders come this way? Would she and Paco be captured again? They would have to find kind people somewhere, find a home where they could live. Bonita longed for a snug barn *now*, before the sun went down again, before the prairie wolves howled.

Bonita stamped a forehoof.

Paco looked up at her for an instant, then went back to grazing, his gray jaw working fast, as though he thought he might never see deep green grass again.

When Paco finally started off once more, Bonita

followed. She kept her head up and her nostrils flared, trying to catch the scents of cooking and cows that would lead her to a rancho. But the wind was empty, washed clean by the open country that stretched to the horizon.

It was a warm day, and the sun beat upon Bonita's back, drying the bloody saddle sore. Still, the flies found it as midday approached, stinging and tickling.

Bonita twitched her skin to scatter them and shook her head—but of course the long, white fly-shooing mane was gone. The loosely circled bridle reins flapped, which did some good, but not enough.

Paco changed direction slightly and Bonita tested the wind, her heart rising. Had he smelled warm stew cooking or a cow pasture? Bonita pulled in long breaths. Nothing. Nothing besides the endless grass and wildflowers. They kept walking.

The flies got worse. They settled onto Bonita's back, ringing the saddle sore. She twitched her skin and shook every step or two. She switched her tail even though she knew it was too short to reach. The flies buzzed and bit no matter what she did. It was maddening.

The sun climbed and the heat was like a weight on Bonita's back. She was miserable. The sky was too big, with vultures wheeling in endless circles, watching for the dead and dying of the dry earth. Mice rustled in the grass and quail bobbed their heads, walking fast to clear the way.

Bonita lowered her head and walked just fast enough to keep up with Paco's short-legged jog-trot.

After a long time, Paco made a deep snorting sound and Bonita looked up. There was a stand of cottonwoods off to the south. Bonita looked longingly at the shade beneath the trees. It wasn't as hot as summer would be later on, but she was tired and bruised and scared.

Paco brayed suddenly and Bonita jerked her head up. His long ears were pointing straight at the cottonwoods now. Bonita half turned, following Paco's stare, afraid that she would see rows of horses pounding toward them.

But there was only one.

A tall lanky palomino walked toward them

across the low early grass and the red-budded amargosa bushes. Bonita recognized him instantly. It was the horse she had seen with María—the young stallion who had been so far ahead of the others that morning on the road to San Antonio. *Raphael.*

Bonita glanced at Paco. He was standing still, with his head lifted to scent the wind. Bonita took a step toward the stallion. Maybe this was his rancho. Maybe his people were kind and fair. She took another step.

Paco shook his stubby mane and stamped a forehoof. Bonita took a third step, looking back at him. Paco struck the ground again, then lowered his ears and trotted to catch up.

Bonita approached the stallion carefully. He was standing still, his ears forward, switching his long smoke-colored tail against the flies. His mane was long, the cascade of smoke and cream falling well below his neck.

As they got closer, Paco trotted out in front of Bonita. Raphael arched his neck, bending until they touched muzzles. Bonita could hear them snuffling in each other's breath, exchanging scents, getting to know each other.

Bonita waited respectfully. When Raphael approached her, she breathed in his breath in exchange for her own. He smelled of sage and chemise brush and sky—he smelled like the wind. He had not been captured; she could smell no scent of human or leather on him at all.

She knew that she smelled of both. And a whiff of skunk still surrounded her. Her head low, Bonita allowed him to sniff at the bridle and bit, then her ragged mane and tail. He gently investigated her wound.

Then he did something unexpected. He leaned across her back and shook his head, shooing the circle of flies away from her wound with his mane. When they buzzed back, he scattered them again. For a long moment he kept it up, freeing her of the stinging itch of the flies for the first time since she had been hurt.

Then he turned and led off.

Bonita fell into step behind Raphael. Paco hesitated, then joined her.

The shade beneath the cottonwoods was deep and cool. There was a shallow creek. Bonita waded in and sucked down long swallows of the water, the bit rubbing against her tongue. Her mouth was sore from it, but her saddle sore and her bruises were so much worse, she barely noticed.

While Paco and Raphael drank, Bonita pawed at the water, soaking her own belly and legs.

Paco stood in the creek for a long moment after he finished drinking. Then he made his way up the bank to graze in the sun. Bonita stayed, Raphael standing close beside her.

The next morning they all woke at sunrise. Under a sky cobbled by pink clouds, Raphael led off. Bonita and Paco followed him through the flat brush country. Bonita slept better that night, standing between Paco and Raphael and hearing their steady breathing, feeling their warmth.

The morning after that, Paco led the way and found a creek before noon. There was little shade, but the water was deep and sweet. Raphael bit Paco playfully and for a moment they splashed in the water like colts. Then Raphael led them onward.

Bonita followed. She didn't know what else to do. They had not seen a rancho or a barn or people in a long time. The prairie around them was as big as the sky above them. She felt small and lost.

Chapter Eight

*S*pring faded into summer. The heat settled in. Every day we would walk until midday, then we tried to find shade to doze. After that we would walk again until evening. Every day I looked for riders, waited for the smell of cooking or cows, watched for a plume of chimney smoke, but still we passed no ranchos. I know now that out of the three of us, I was the only one hoping we would find people to care for us. Paco and Raphael were making sure we didn't....

Every morning, colors spilled into the clouds as the sun lifted itself above them. There were deep pinks and hazy oranges that faded and brightened until the sky was clear and blue, an arched dome that made Bonita feel tiny.

At first the feeling made her long for her stall, but as the days passed, she began to miss it less. She had never seen a sunrise from inside the adobe barn. Or a sunset. And even though Juan had kept her bucket clean, the water had never tasted as clean and sweet as the clear cool water in the creeks they found, one after another, as they headed northwest.

Bonita's bruises healed and the saddle sore closed and scarred over. The bridle remained a misery, the bit always in the way of eating and drinking, but Bonita sometimes forgot it was there for an hour or two.

By midday, the summer sun was fierce. The heat shimmered upward from the soil, as though the earth had had enough and wanted to throw it back at the sun. Everything was gilded, bright, and dry. The wildflowers were long gone and the grass was stiff and thick-stemmed.

Nudging Bonita ahead of him, Raphael climbed

out of a creek, water streaming from his coat as he followed her up the steep bank.

He stopped beside a cottonwood and rubbed his jaw on the rough bark, scratching himself. He turned his head slightly, rubbing one ear, then the other, on the tree trunk.

Bonita watched, then joined him. It felt wonderful, almost as good as being brushed. She rubbed harder, twisting her neck to scratch the poll of her head. As she worked to reach the skin beneath the bridle strap, she felt it slide, bending her right ear forward.

Startled, she tossed her head and the bridle slid loose on the right side.

Raphael was scrubbing at his own itches, his eyes closed as Bonita shook her head, hard. The bridle's loosened headstall flopped, this time freeing her other ear.

The bit dropped, clinking her teeth hard enough to make her open her mouth. The bridle slid to the ground.

Startled, then delighted, Bonita nudged Raphael.

He opened his eyes and stared at her, then lowered his head to sniff at the fallen bridle.

Stepping past it carefully, as though it were something dangerous, he led her farther down the bank to get away from it. Bonita looked back once. The bridle lay there, the reins curved like snakes in the sand.

Bonita rubbed her jaw against the inside of her foreleg, feeling the sting where the bit had rubbed her skin raw. She nibbled a little grass and chewed it slowly, wondering at the pleasure of eating without the bit pinning down her tongue.

Stopping beneath another wide-branched cottonwood, Raphael reached out to groom Bonita, blowing warm breath against her cheek. Then he stood easily, his weight on one hind hoof, the other tipped up. Bonita positioned herself beside him and for a time they daydreamed side by side.

Raphael closed his eyes. Bonita listened to the birds in the trees, the buzz of dragonflies over the creek. She felt better than she had in all the days since the battle. The hateful bridle was finally gone.

Her mouth would soon heal from the constant bruising of the bit.

And Raphael smelled of sweet grass and dust and clear water—not fear. He dozed, his eyes closing in the deep shade of the cottonwoods. Bonita looked up. Overhead, a breeze stirred the leaves and they flashed like silver coins.

Days later they stood on a hillside and watched three thunderstorms pass in the distance. The rain fell in a dove-gray column beneath the cloud. On every side of the rain, the sun shone brightly.

As they stood watching, Bonita saw that one of the storms was headed straight for them, sweeping across the land faster than hawk-flight.

Paco lifted his head and brayed at the rain. Bonita glanced around. There was no shelter in sight, no rock ledges, no trees. The thorny scrub brush and sage were unbroken all the way to the circle of the horizon. Bonita inhaled deeply and Paco brayed again, then danced in a tight circle.

Raphael pawed the ground, then kicked his heels

at the air, swinging his tail in a grand arc. Bonita felt her skin prickle as the rain came closer.

She could smell it, the sharp metallic scent of water mixed with bruised sage and wet grass. The wind kicked up tufts of sand and spun itself into dust devils that skittered past, driven ahead of the coming storm.

Bonita pawed at the ground.

Paco brayed.

Raphael whinnied low and long, challenging the rain that was rushing toward them, darkening the sky. The clouds were suddenly overhead, snuffing out the sun in an instant.

Then the rain hit them, big drops pelting down that soaked them to the skin. Lightning flashed, and the blue-white light transformed the world. An instant later thunder rumbled and crashed.

Raphael reared and squealed, striking at the storm, pretending to fight the very air that surrounded them. Paco leaped and bucked, the rain soaking his thick coat flat, turning it the color of the clouds.

Bonita stood trembling as the lightning flashed

again. This time the thunder was so loud that she felt the rumbling crash flow into her hooves, into her bones.

Bonita flinched, desperate to free herself of the earth, of the strange vibration in the soil—but too scared to move. She wanted to be back in her dry, straw-bedded stall. She stood rigid as the sky overhead crackled with lightning again. Thunder followed an instant later.

The rain that soaked through her coat was cold and she shook, huddling close to a tall thicket of chemise brush.

Raphael reared in the eerie, blue-white light, then sprang downhill, galloping. Paco lunged after him. They ran in a long circle, then came back up the slope, both of them soaked and dripping.

They slid to a halt beside Bonita and Raphael tilted his head, dodging to one side like a foal at play. Then he leaped close and shook himself, the water from his coat spraying Bonita. Paco lifted his head and brayed, then he shook, too.

Bonita shook her own mane, but it was too short,

too uneven to repay them. She stamped one forehoof and glared at Raphael. He acted as though he had no idea why she was upset, sidling closer, nipping at her shoulder playfully.

Bonita nudged him away with her muzzle, but he pushed her right back. He shook his mane again and Bonita reared, dancing backward to get out of the way. He was acting like a colt.

The rain was pouring down now and Bonita was drenched, her white coat plastered flat against her skin. Raphael shook his dripping mane again. Bonita lifted one foreleg to strike the ground. Then she pretended to nip at him. He pretended to nip back. Then he wheeled around and galloped away. Paco followed him and Bonita leaped into a gallop to chase them both.

The rain seemed to wash away Bonita's fear as she raced to catch up. In twenty strides she had passed Paco, but Raphael's long legs and natural speed—and his head start—kept him in the lead.

Bonita glanced back to see Paco slowing to buck, arching his back against the veins of lightning overhead. Then she concentrated on catching Raphael.

With the thirsty prairie beneath her hooves and lightning sparking overhead, Bonita pounded after him, stretching out and galloping hard. The ground blurred beneath her hooves and she found herself leaping sagebrush rather than skirting it.

Lightning struck close by a second time and Bonita threw herself forward, galloping faster than she ever had in her life.

In front of her, she saw Raphael slowing, veering to one side. As Bonita shifted her course to follow him, she realized he was making a wide, plunging turn, circling back.

She angled toward him and they met, straightening their courses to run side by side. They galloped together, their necks outstretched, their hoofbeats lost in the roar of rain and sky.

Bonita saw Raphael flatten out, reaching, trying to outrun her. She lengthened her own stride and kept up, a wild joy rising in her heart. Lightning flickered in the clouds, a crackling web that blinked into life, then went out.

As the storm passed overhead they burst into the sunshine at the edge of its shadow and went on, jumping a creek, then charging up the bank of the far side. A rib of jutting red rock seamed the earth and they soared over it, then galloped on in unison.

Bonita felt light, as though she had wings instead of hooves. The ground seemed to roll under her while she stayed in one place. The sun shone on her wet back, warming her. She wanted to gallop forever.

It was Raphael who slowed first. Bonita matched her stride to his, breaking back into a trot, then slowing to a walk. They topped a ridge and stood in the sun. Heaving in huge breaths of the rain-washed air, they watched the storm fly away, across the sagebrush prairie. Bonita pranced, joyous, breath-less. Her longest, wildest gallops with Maria had never made her feel like this.

Paco was coming toward them, clattering along in his stiff-legged gallop, braying at them for leaving him behind. Bonita stood looking out at the huge sky and for the first time she didn't feel small and scared beneath it. She felt safe—and *free*.

Two days after the rain, they saw columns of riders like the ones who had captured Bonita. They were dressed alike and covered with road dust and they were riding their horses hard.

Bonita was trembling as Raphael guided them down into a ravine and the riders passed without seeing them. The next day, Raphael led them westward again and Bonita was glad. She did not want to live anywhere near these men.

Summer ended with a furnace blast of heat, each day seeming hotter than the one before it. One morning, Bonita stood beside Paco as he lifted his head and bared his teeth. He faced west, then turned northward, still curling his upper lip back.

Bonita had seen him do it before, but this time she imitated him.

After a moment, Paco started off.

Raphael looked up from his grazing, then followed, glancing back at Bonita. She stood for a second longer, her lip curled, facing north as Paco had.

What was it the burro had smelled that decided the direction to take?

Bonita pulled in a long breath through her open mouth and held it, startled. There, as faint as moon shadows, was a scent she knew well.

Water.

Bonita followed Paco and Raphael. As the morning wore on, they could see the line of trees along the distant creek. Raphael tossed his head and picked up the pace and Bonita knew that he was smelling the water for the first time.

The next afternoon, Bonita faced into the breeze and bared her teeth.

She saw Paco staring at her. He didn't bray, but he switched his short tail back and forth. Bonita pulled in a long slow breath.

The scent was even fainter today, but she was sure of it. Without waiting for Paco or Raphael, she led off. And when she turned to look back, she saw them both following her. All the rushing joy of the rainstorm came back into her heart. She was free—and she could find water without help!

Chapter Nine

*G*alloping on windy ridges with Raphael, I was not afraid. I was strong. The sky was no longer too big. Barns had become too small. We saw the dark-coated riders three more times. Every time, we avoided them and moved on.

The nights were getting chilly and the country was changing. Cliffs of red rock lined the curves of dry riverbeds. Hills were layered with colors—white, gray, and red rock exposed by the ancient winds.

It was getting harder to find water and shelter. And a disturbing thing began to happen. Once every day or two they crossed trails that wound through the brush—and these paths carried old scents of cattle and cowboys.

Bonita began to listen for hoofbeats and whoops, but for a different reason than before. She didn't want to find men, she wanted to avoid them. Raphael and Paco were constantly on watch. As they grazed, they faced away from each other, lifting their heads every few seconds to scan opposite horizons.

Bonita lay down each night, pawing herself up a bed of looser, softer soil, but then lay awake listening and scenting the wind most of the night. The sighing air brought news of cows, and men, but it was always old news. Still, she could tell that it made Raphael uneasy and knew they would not stay long near these scents.

Traveling every day from dawn to dusk, they saw no cattle, no human beings, but they kept coming across the cow-scented trails that wound between the red-rock mesas. It bothered Bonita. A place was either a rancho or it was not. If cattle had lived here earlier in the year, where had they gone? Where were the men who had driven them along the trails?

Bonita woke one morning to see something she had never seen before. Without waking Raphael or Paco, she stood facing west, shivering in the morning chill, staring at the horizon. All of her life, the sky had met the land in a smooth curve along gentle hills or endless flatlands.

At the limit of her vision, Bonita could see jagged hills, topped with white. They were so far away that mist blurred their tops. How high did a hill have to be to disappear into the sky? Bonita shook her mane. These were mountains, she was sure— *la sierra*, María had called them.

"YEE-up!!!"

The shout brought Paco and Raphael plunging to their feet. Bonita spun in a circle, startled witless. Riding toward them at a dead gallop were a pack of cowboys, their lariats coiled and ready.

"Watch the stud horse!" one of them shouted. "Some of these mustangs will come right at you."

"I want the white mare!" one of his friends shouted back.

Several of the men laughed and shouted taunts.

Before Bonita could move, Paco was skittering to the side, his legs working furiously as he galloped off at an angle.

"Get 'em all!" one of the men yelled.

An instant later, a lariat floated out in a perfect toss, circling Paco's neck. The smart little burro slid to a stop before it could drag him down. Then he stood, his head down. The cowboy laughed, swinging off his horse. "This one isn't so wild!"

It happened in seconds. Raphael bit at Bonita's shoulder, startling her into leaping forward. Together they galloped, hurtling over the ground, going faster and faster.

Raphael matched her speed and they left the cow ponies behind. In the distance, Bonita saw the mountains. They looked beautiful and far away—and safe.

"Let 'em go! One of the cowboys shouted. "We've got cows to push north!"

There were shouted answers from his friends, but the drumming of Bonita's own hooves drowned them out.

By dusk, she and Raphael stood side by side on a hilltop, hidden by a stand of sage and buck brush. Around midnight, Bonita led the way upwind, then angled back across the breeze, scenting the wind.

Paco's scent was as familiar to Bonita as her own skin and once she found it, she turned into the wind to follow it. Raphael trailed behind her, reluctant to backtrack toward danger, but keeping up.

They walked through the night, Bonita leading the way. She knew what Paco would do if he couldn't escape. He would fight. And the cowboys wouldn't like it.

Sunrise pinked the horizon and when the first light shot across the endless prairie, Bonita slowed.

It wasn't hard to find the cowboys. The smell of bacon frying carried easily across sagebrush and wild grass. The smell of unwashed men and hundreds of cows came with it.

Raphael saw them first. He stopped and tossed his head, whickering low in his throat, so quietly that

Bonita turned, expecting to see him tense and afraid. But he wasn't. Raphael was shaking with rage.

He pawed at the ground, then started forward, snaking a path through the brush. Bonita followed, resisting the urge to whinny, to let Paco know they were close. He was dozing, she saw, probably tired from a night of rope fighting.

The cowboys were circled around their fire. Two leaned forward, passing plates back and forth, eating in silence. Bonita could hear their knives ticking against the tin plates. The rest were sitting back, their legs stretched out in front of them, dozing with their hats low or picking their teeth with sage twigs.

Bonita stepped lightly, staying close behind Raphael. Beyond the camp, the cattle were shifting, grazing. It was a big herd, mostly patchy-colored longhorns. They were bawling and grunting, restless for better, untrampled grass. A few men rode in lazy circles around the herd, their horses ambling with their heads low.

Closer to them, there was a group of small saddle horses; a rope corral had been strung between the buck brush and sage, strengthened by metal stakes. Just beyond it, Paco was tied close, hitched to another stout stake driven into the ground.

By the time one of the men looked up, Bonita and Raphael had made their way close to the corral that enclosed the horses.

"Hoppin' John and brimstone, look at that!" the cowboy shouted.

The rest of the men scrambled to their feet and stood, staring. Then one man grabbed up his saddle and saddle blanket and ran toward the horses. Off to the side, Paco woke and began to bray. Raphael reared and the horses crowded away from him, pushing on the rope fence.

Paco backed up, straining against his tether.

It snapped.

Bonita knew then why Paco had slept past dawn. He had spent the night chewing at the tough fiber.

"They've come back to us, boys," the man carrying his saddle shouted. He grabbed his mare's halter and laughed.

The others scrambled for their tack, but it was too late. Raphael stepped forward. Bonita watched him nervously. He had his head low, his neck stretched out parallel to the ground. His ears were flat against his head and his eyes were narrowed. Abruptly, he charged the horses, squealing a challenge that pierced the quiet dawn.

Bonita reared, wheeling in a half turn, startled. Paco gathered his balance and sprang into a gallop, his short legs carrying him away at an angle.

Raphael hit the rope and kept going, dragging it free of the sage and metal stakes. The horses milled in a circle, a few lifting their heads, realizing the fence was down. Then they focused on Raphael, coming at them with his head low. They slammed into each other, frantic to get away. The single cowboy who had managed to saddle up turned to shout at the herd riders.

Then everything blurred. Bonita saw the mounted cowboys coming toward Raphael at a gallop. One of them had drawn his gun. Scared for Raphael, Bonita lunged forward.

"Don't shoot," someone yelled. "That mare is bloodstock!"

Bonita wheeled around. The mounted cowboy

was starting after the loosed saddle horses. Paco was galloping away, headed straight across open country.

The cowboy held his gun steady. "If he doesn't attack us, let him go. You can't tame a horse like that."

Raphael reared once more, then, whinnying at Bonita, he spun around and galloped after Paco. Bonita lunged after him. Strung out behind them rode three cursing cowboys. The others shouted and shook their fists from the camp.

Bonita saw Raphael reach Paco and slow down. In an instant, she knew he would turn to face their pursuers as they got closer.

Veering hard to the side, Bonita slowed to a canter.

"That mare isn't as wild as the other two," one of the men shouted.

"We could sell her in Denver," another shouted.

"First man to get a rope on her owns her," a third voice yelled.

There were no shouts after that. All three riders turned their mounts to follow Bonita. She hit her stride again, but didn't run flat out. She kept looking to make sure Raphael and Paco kept going. She knew it would take time before Raphael realized she wasn't following him.

Bonita flattened out, galloping harder, then glanced back. Two of the horses had been riding herd all night and the third had a choppy gait that would tire him fast. And none of them knew what she now knew.

She could pick her way through rocky, horse-crippling country at a dead gallop. She knew she could find water and grass and shelter. A rising sense of her own strength made Bonita's hooves fly over the ground. She was free. She no longer needed people to survive.

Bonita was far enough ahead by noon to sneak a drink at a spring she had smelled on the wind. She burst out of the brush and led her pursuers past it. Their horses, she knew, would tire faster if they were thirsty.

By midafternoon, two of the horses had fallen so far back that she couldn't see them. She dropped down into a narrow canyon and followed a dry creek bed far enough to find a little green grass. Hidden in the bushes, she grazed while the remaining cowboy rode back and forth, trying to follow her tracks on the gravel-covered ground.

After she had rested, she galloped off again, startling him once again as she thundered past. He whooped and lashed his horse with the reins, a grim look on his face.

It was almost sunset before Bonita heard the cowboy curse and rein in his exhausted horse. She was tired, too, sweat foaming on her shoulders and flanks. But when the rider started back at a walk, she found her spirits soaring. She had done it! She had escaped three riders and she had kept her freedom! Tossing her head, she began a long, wide turn.

Under a rising full moon, Bonita slowed to a canter but kept going, lifting her head to taste the wind. When she finally caught the scents she was hoping for, she whinnied.

Ahead of her, his long ears silvered in the moonlight, Paco brayed back. Raphael tossed his head and his smoke-white mane fanned out as he broke into a gallop. Bonita danced into a canter, all the weariness of the long journey vanishing at the sight of him.

They all three stood close together for a long time, their shoulders touching, nuzzling and grooming each other until Bonita calmed down enough to fall asleep. She woke twice to find Raphael alert, his head up as he watched and listened for danger.

At sunrise they went on again, keeping watch behind themselves. They traveled faster, grazing as they went. Every day the mountains were closer, and so was winter. A few blustery days told Bonita why Raphael didn't want to be on the plains when the big storms of winter howled across the land. The biting autumn winds were terrible. A real storm could kill them out in the open like this.

Chapter Ten

I think Raphael was hoping we could cross the mountains before the weather got too bad, then descend the other side to live in foothills far from cowboys and fighting. But he had no idea how these mountains lined up, one range hiding behind another. Our coats grew long. Paco's grew thick, like sheep's wool. The snow fell for hours, then did not melt as it had back in San Antonio. It lay in layers. Raphael taught us to eat willow bark. It was bitter but we got used to it. All we could do was keep going. Paco and I faltered, many times. Raphael never did.

Bonita hated the way the snow collapsed beneath her hooves, the way it scraped at her belly when they had to move to find more willow. Sometimes, Raphael had to nip at her to get her to flounder through the snow.

Paco's fuzzy coat kept him warm, but the thick whiskers on his muzzle caught the moisture from his breath and formed a mass of tiny icicles that he was always trying to rub off on the rough bark of the pine trees. Balls of snow built up in the hollow underside of their hooves, making them clumsy and awkward even where the snow wasn't deep.

One morning Bonita awakened to see that the whole world was now white. Above them was a summit without pine trees, without a single living thing that she could see. No dark rocks jutted through the deep snow. Even the sky was gray-white. Driven along by hunger, they kept climbing.

Paco led the way. Bonita followed him and Raphael walked behind her on the narrow trails. Following a steep path along the side of a mountain, Bonita stumbled, staring down at the rocky gorge below. Raphael rested his muzzle on her back for a moment, until she steadied herself, then they went on.

The trail wound along the brink of the drop-off for hours and Bonita's courage was failing again when, suddenly, from above them, a sliding trickle of snow spilled downward.

Bonita looked up, startled, and saw three animals with horns that curled in tight circles along the sides of their heads. Their coats were cream white, like sheep, but when they leaped from one rock to another, Bonita stared. They seemed to be able to find footing where the snow itself couldn't cling.

Bonita followed the narrow trail with less fear after that. She placed her feet with more faith. The sheep with curving horns had made the path they were following, she was sure. And they seemed to know how to make their way in these mountains.

One evening, standing huddled with Raphael for warmth, Bonita sensed something changing inside herself, something deep and mysterious. She didn't know what the feeling meant.

Bonita knew what she wanted. She wanted a home—a place where she knew where to find food and water—a place she knew was safe.

A howling snowstorm pinned them in a shallow valley for four days. They stood close together to ease the cold, and Bonita ate only a little willow bark and some lichen from the rocks, scraping her teeth along the stone.

When the wind finally stopped, Raphael led them upward again. A fiercely bright sun glittered on the wind-polished snow, blinding Bonita with its glare. The path was covered in drifted snow now, but a single set of sheep tracks marked its course across the steep slope.

As they walked, Bonita's stomach ached. She was so hungry. She had never known it was possible to be this hungry. Her empty belly clawed at her courage, and she fell behind. Raphael stopped more than once to wait for her. When the trail widened into a high valley, he walked beside her, nudging her along. When the trail narrowed again, he dropped back behind her.

They stopped in a tiny valley and chewed willow bark until dusk. It did not satisfy Bonita's hunger, but the aching diminished for a while at least.

That night they heard a mountain lion's grating roar. The sound battered its way down the gorge. Bonita trembled with fear.

Raphael started awake and Bonita heard him pulling in drafts of the thin air, trying to catch a scent of the big cat, trying to tell how close it was.

They all three stood awake, listening, until the sun rose and they could start down the trail once more. It was a spectacular sunrise and Bonita and Raphael stood shoulder to shoulder watching the birth of the new day. The sky was clear again and the first shafts of daylight turned the shadowy snow into a sparkling expanse of white.

It was cold, colder than it had ever been. Bonita didn't want to travel, but there was nothing more to eat in the narrow valley, so they had to go on. Paco led the way and Bonita followed him. Raphael brought up the rear, watching for the mountain lion, ready to protect Bonita and Paco.

They walked steadily as the sun climbed the curve of the sky. All morning, the trail cut across a steep slope, following the base of dark cliffs. As the sun started its downward slant, the cliffs ended and the trail was bounded on both sides by unbroken sheets of deep snow.

Bonita heard a rumbling sound and tossed her head up. Was it a bear's growl? Raphael stopped and looked back, then glanced up the slope.

He lunged forward, biting Bonita's flank, hard. Confused and startled, she plunged forward, stumbling into Paco. The burro shoved his way through a chest-deep snowdrift, trying to get out of Bonita's way.

Raphael lunged again, striking at Bonita's legs with his forehoof, reaching to nip at her flanks, trumpeting a desperate whinny. Bonita broke into a snow-clumsy canter, terrified of the drop down into the chasm, but even more afraid of the rumbling sound behind her.

A sudden rush of wind slammed into her side and Bonita nearly fell, then managed to stay upright and to keep up her flailing canter, following Paco away from the terrible sound. It was growing, swelling to fill her ears, her world. Then, somehow, it got even louder.

Behind them came a crashing roar, a sound so loud it seemed the very earth must be shifting, sliding toward the chasm. It shrieked and groaned as though the mountain itself had been horribly wounded and was crying out in pain.

Then, abruptly, the mountain went silent. The silence was as terrifying as the roar and Bonita galloped on, clambering after Paco, afraid to slow down. When she finally broke back into a trot, then stopped to look back, what she saw seemed impossible.

The snow had formed a rushing river that had coursed downhill, taking everything with it. The pine trees downslope had been snapped in half, boulders had been moved. The churned, dirty snow had filled the chasm and had splashed up the far side, shooting into the air.

Bonita started back, following her own ragged

tracks, her muzzle close to the snow, trying to catch a scent of Raphael. Paco followed her.

Finally, they could go no farther. They stood together, staring at the place where her tracks ended, where the river of falling snow had swept downward.

Bonita whinnied, over and over.

Paco brayed, his grating call echoing off the mountainside.

Raphael did not answer.

He could not, Bonita realized.

Raphael was gone forever.

Chapter Eleven

*A*t first I wasn't sure I wanted to live without Raphael. But Paco kept me moving. He stood next to me at night and every day pawed away at the crusted snow to uncover frozen grass for us to eat. There was something deep inside me that cried out for more food, for warmer days and gentler country. Paco and I kept going. The trail soon started downward.

The weather got warmer and warmer as Bonita and Paco came down out of the high peaks. The snow thinned. The sheep trail ended, but they found others that smelled of deer and bear and led downward through pines and scattered meadows.

The days grew longer, warmer. One morning, Bonita saw a pair of blue jays carrying bits of grass straw in their beaks and knew that spring had come. It was that same day she felt a fluttering movement inside her belly, as though a butterfly had become trapped there. She didn't know what it meant, but it made her stop more often to graze on the new green grass that was rising out of the snow-patched ground.

A few days later, they came down from the foothills onto the plains. The ground was a riot of seedlings, each little plant stretching toward the sun.

It rained one afternoon and Bonita bucked like a yearling filly, galloping back and forth until Paco finally joined her, the raindrops spattering off their backs. She thought about Raphael and she was pretty sure that Paco was remembering his good friend, too, as they ran in the warm rain. Raphael had taught them both to feel free.

Bonita's heart was healing. Rain meant spring and spring meant summer and deep grass and sleeping without shuddering in a cold wind. She would never again cross the mountains in winter. She would find a home and stay there.

Paco was the first to see the horses. He made an odd sound, as though his breath had caught. Bonita lifted her head to see him standing stiffly, his long ears slanted forward. She followed his gaze and blinked in surprise.

There were sorrels and bays and palominos among the horses, as well as a number of pintos. And she could see that several of the mares had swollen bellies like the ones that had been kept, waiting to foal, in the stall across the aisle from hers. All of them were chewing, their mouths full of green grass.

The memory of the stall, and María, seemed distant and blurred, like something seen at dusk. But as she thought about the mares and the way they had eaten every scrap of hay, she suddenly understood something about herself. The fluttering inside her was a foal. This idea was so amazing—and so wonderful—that Bonita closed her eyes for a few seconds.

Paco nudged her shoulder and Bonita left her daydreaming to look at him. He was starting forward, his ears up and his eyes wide. Bonita followed him, eager to meet these horses, to graze near them.

She could see a few early foals, still spindle-legged and downy and wide-eyed. Bonita looked at their mothers. Surely these mares knew how to live in this place, knew where the creeks were and where to find grass if the rain failed and where the mountain lions stalked and everything else she needed to learn.

The herd's stallion trotted toward them, his neck arched. He was a heavily built horse the color of evening shadows—not black, but not brown or gray either. He circled them once, then again.

Bonita and Paco stood still, waiting for him to approach them. He moved like a shadow, too, Bonita thought, sweeping across the ground. His gait was perfectly cadenced.

Shadow approached Bonita first. He took in her breath and blew his own, sweet with new grass, across her face. Then he lowered his head to touch Paco's muzzle with his own.

Shadow shook his mane and returned to the herd. Bonita felt her heart rising. They had found horses to live with, a stallion who would protect them.

Bonita started to follow Shadow, but before she had taken more than a few steps, a pinto mare came forward, staring at her intently. It was not a friendly stare. The mare had a nearly white face—all but the lower part of her muzzle, which was a deep honey color. The rest of her body was patched with shapes like white clouds on an amber sky.

Bonita stopped and grazed, keeping her distance, eating a few mouthfuls of grass. Then she started forward again. The mare advanced a step as well, facing Bonita squarely. Bonita stopped again. The mare was telling her clearly that she was not welcome—not yet.

Every day Paco and Bonita grazed near—but not

too near—the herd. Shadow would sometimes come to stand by them, grazing and then lifting his head to listen and scent the wind for danger. But the lead mare never came close. And if Bonita carelessly grazed past an invisible line, the mare appeared, her ears flat and her stance square and head-on.

Whenever it happened, Bonita would walk a few steps away, then fall to eating again. If the pinto mare went back to her own grazing, Bonita knew she had retreated far enough. If not, she took a few more steps away from the herd.

Bonita's hunger amazed her. She grazed every minute of every day and still she was hungry. The grass grew thick and sweet and she knew she was lucky. It would be terrible to need extra food for an unborn foal and not be able to find it. Her belly continued to swell and Paco sometimes groomed her back—she could no longer reach around to do it herself.

One day a violent rainstorm drove all the horses beneath a stand of cottonwood trees. Bonita and Paco stayed off to one side and the lead mare tolerated their presence. Bonita found herself staring at the foals that shivered in the storm, standing close to their mothers. When the sun came out again, the lead mare faced Bonita, forcing her to back away once more.

When the herd moved, Bonita and Paco followed them. Shadow let the pinto lead mare decide which paths to follow, and when to leave them. He walked behind the herd, usually, so Bonita and Paco often would end up following him, a little distance away.

They were walking in a gully one day, using its steep sides to avoid a stinging wind, when clouds topped the mountains behind them and slid downward, gray and dark. The rain, when it came, was as heavy as hail, big, round drops that fell in dense sheets.

Bonita walked with her back humped and her head low, wishing the lead mare would leave the gully and find some trees to break the pelting rainfall. She didn't.

The rain kept on, the storm clouds pouring over the mountainous divide. The gully began to run with water stained red from the color of the soil.

Bonita saw Paco stop and turn and a second later, she heard an odd noise coming from behind them. Paco brayed suddenly and leaped for the steep bank. He scrambled up. Bonita, used to heeding Paco's warnings, scrambled after him, squealing an alarm. She had no idea what the danger was, but it was coming, and fast. She made it out of the gully, then stood on the bank looking down at the herd, her sides heaving.

Shadow suddenly threw his head up and charged forward, running alongside his mares, biting at them, trumpeting frantically. Most of them wheeled around to escape Shadow's fury and found themselves facing the steep bank. The lead mare reacted first, clambering upward on the nearly vertical bank, whinnying urgently.

The mares began to follow her example. Bonita pawed the earth nervously. The sound was getting louder and Bonita realized what it was.

Water.

The rainstorm had spilled enough rain to fill the little gully and the water was racing down it fast enough to roar.

From where she stood on the high bank, Bonita could see logs and branches caught in the wall of muddy water.

Bonita pawed and whinnied, urging the mares to hurry upward to safety. Paco danced in a circle, braying over and over, the grating sound echoing back from the foothills.

The water swept closer, then, suddenly, it was upon them. A bay mare got caught in the rush of brown water, but managed to swim back to the current's edge, struggling up and out of the gully. Her foal was less lucky. Squealing and screaming it was washed along with the flood, swept far downstream in an instant.

Bonita heard the anguished scream of the foal's mother. It touched her heart. How terrible it would be to carry a foal, then birth it, then lose it in an instant like this.

The foal answered, its neighing high-pitched and terrified. Bonita was high enough on the bank to see it struggling to keep its head above water as the flash flood shoved it downstream.

Bonita whirled and galloped flat out along the bank, racing the swift water that carried the foal. It was swimming strongly—the current was just too much for it.

Bonita stretched out, pounding over the ground, until she was even with the foal. She leaped over the roots of a fallen tree that spanned the gully just as the colt was washed against its branches. Bonita plunged down the steep bank, whinnying frantically.

The foal, confused and terrified, suddenly focused on her, and struggled free of the branches. It swam desperately, fighting for every inch.

Bonita braved the swift water, wading in, reaching out to touch the foal as it swam bravely to her, then standing between the foal and the raging current downstream until it hit the shallows and could stand.

As the foal staggered out of the muddy water, shaking and clumsy, Bonita turned and nudged it up the slope. She scrambled up the muddy bank after the foal—and found herself face-to-face with the lead mare.

Bonita braced herself, sure the mare would attack her for coming so close to the foal. But the lead mare only stared at her. Then, after a long moment, she half turned, her body angled in a way that made it clear that Bonita could pass her without trouble.

Bonita heard the foal's mother calling and nudged him toward her. Inside her body, Raphael's foal moved a little and she glanced up at the mountains, remembering him, remembering how he had protected her.

Then she walked past the lead mare.

Bonita knew she was home. She had earned her place in the herd. The horses touched her muzzle one by one. They took her breath and gave her their own. And when it came time to move on, Paco and Bonita walked side by side with the others.

Chapter Twelve

*R*aphael's daughter came into the world on the most beautiful afternoon. Everything in the world looked new that day. I have never forgotten a single instant of it.

Bonita awoke feeling different, knowing that her foal was coming soon. By midmorning, she knew her time was close. Heaving in a breath, walking heavily, she went past the lead mare, stopping to exchange a breath with the steady, cautious older horse. Then she walked away from the herd into a stand of pines.

Paco saw her leave and followed her. He stood outside the copse of trees, but stayed close as the hours passed and Bonita's labor began.

At midday, when the lead mare would have usually moved the herd to fresh grass, she did not. Shadow walked back and forth, coming close enough to the pines to hear Bonita's small sounds of labor, then moved off again, satisfied that everything was going as it should.

When the foal was finally born, Bonita wondered at the little filly. She was a pinto, a beautiful red sorrel patched with snowy white. Bonita stared at her a long time, amazed at her perfect tiny hooves, and her bright, wide eyes.

As the foal stood up for the first time, rocking back and forth on her long legs, blinking, her long eyelashes brushing her face, Bonita named her.

Sierra.

It was Maria's word for the high mountain of her girlhood home. It was a high mountain where Sierra's father had been lost saving her life. It seemed perfect.

Bonita heard hooves shifting on the sandy soil and looked out of the trees. Paco and the rest of the horses were grazing close by, waiting.

Bonita got to her feet slowly, feeling weary but light of heart. She moved forward, watching her foal. Wobbling, but walking with her head held high, Sierra followed her mother out of the trees. Every horse in the herd stopped grazing and turned to welcome her.

Other *SPIRIT OF THE CIMARRON* titles:

SIERRA
ESPERANZA
SPIRIT